The Case Of

CAMP CROOKED LAKE

Look for more great books in

series:

The Case Of
CAMP CROOKED LAKE

by Carol Ellis

HarperEntertainment
An Imprint of HarperCollinsPublishers

A PARACHUTE PRESS BOOK

PARACHUTE PRESS

Parachute Publishing, L.L.C.
156 Fifth Avenue
New York, NY 10010

DUALSTAR PUBLICATIONS

Dualstar Publications
c/o Thorne and Company
A Professional Law Corporation
1801 Century Park East
Los Angeles, CA 90067

HarperEntertainment

An Imprint of HarperCollins*Publishers*
10 East 53rd Street, New York, NY 10022

First printing: July 2002

Printed in the United States of America

10 9 8 7 6 5 4 3 2 1

1

START YOUR SUMMER!

"**W**elcome to Camp Crooked Lake!" Mrs. Clancy said with a big smile. "Are you ready for an awesome summer vacation?"

"Bring it on!" My twin sister, Ashley, and I cheered and clapped along with the other campers.

A few hours ago we were at home, packing our bags. Now here we were at the coolest summer camp ever.

"Look at how many activities there are for us to do!" Ashley said, reading from the brochure. "Canoeing, sailing…"

"I can't wait to go swimming!" I cut in. "I want to practice my backstroke, my butterfly—"

"Your zigzag!" Ashley added.

Zigzag? I glanced over at the twisty lake behind the main lodge. "Wow! Check out all its curves. No wonder they named it Crooked Lake!"

"That's one mystery we won't need to solve." Ashley grinned.

I laughed. Ashley and I are detectives. We run the Olsen and Olsen Detective Agency from the attic of our house. But we weren't at Camp Crooked Lake to take on a case. We were here to kick back and have fun!

"Can you believe that Mr. and Mrs. Clancy have been running the camp for over twenty-five years?" Ashley asked.

"That makes"—I pretended to count on my fingers—"fifty thousand roasted marshmallows!"

"Campers, it's time to meet your counselors," Mrs. Clancy called out. "Each group will have their own senior and junior counselors staying in their cabins."

She gestured to four kids wearing bright yellow T-shirts with "Camp Crooked Lake" printed across the front. They all looked about sixteen years old.

"These are your senior counselors," Mrs. Clancy said. "Meet April, Sandi, Dave, and Mike."

The counselors smiled and waved to the group.

"The junior counselors are making sure everything is ready for you back at the cabins," Mrs. Clancy went on. "You'll meet them a little later."

"Mrs. Clancy seems really nice!" I said to Ashley.

But then Mr. Clancy stepped forward and held up one hand. He had a huge frown on his face.

"Breaking the rules will get you into big trouble," Mr. Clancy barked. "No swimming or hiking alone, no boating without a life jacket, no loud music or running around after lights-out, no shouting…"

"What a grouch!" I whispered. "You'd think this was the army—not summer camp."

Ashley shrugged. "Maybe he's just super-serious about the rules," she said.

That's Ashley for you. She never jumps to conclusions about people the way I do.

My sister and I look alike on the outside. We both have strawberry-blond hair and blue eyes. But on the inside we're very different. Ashley always thinks things through carefully. I like to trust my gut feelings. And my gut told me that Mr. Clancy was grumpy about more than just rules!

"Okay, it's time to split up!" Mrs. Clancy said. "April, why don't you call your group first."

A girl with short blond hair stepped forward. "Mary-Kate, Ashley, Vicki, and Kimberly, you're all in Blackbird Cabin!" she said. "Grab your stuff and join me up here."

Ashley and I dragged our sleeping bags and backpacks over to April. Two other girls did the same thing.

"Welcome!" April said. "The four of you will be rooming together for the next two weeks. I'll be your senior counselor. Why don't you all introduce yourselves?"

"I'm Kimberly." One of the girls smiled. She wore her brown hair in a ponytail and had braces on her teeth. "This is my first year at camp."

"I'm Ashley and this is my sister, Mary-Kate," Ashley said.

"We've been to a bunch of camps," I added, "but this seems like the coolest one yet!"

"I'm Vicki," a girl with curly red hair

piped up. "And I'll bet I've been to more camps than you have!"

"That's cool," I said. But who was keeping score?

"Let's go to the cabin now," April suggested. "Joy, your junior counselor, is there waiting for us. This is her first summer at Camp Crooked Lake, too."

"How many summers have you been here?" I asked.

"This is my fifth year," April replied. "Every summer I have the greatest time. I'm sure you'll have a blast, too."

"What do we do first?" Kimberly asked as April led us down a trail. "Volleyball? Swim? Arts and crafts?"

"First you unpack," April told her. "There's a big cookout tonight. But before that we'll go down to the lake for the big canoe race!"

"A race?" Ashley asked excitedly.

April nodded. "Every summer the first-year campers kick off the camp activities with a race to get Mr. Codsworth!"

"Mr. Codsworth?" I asked slowly. "Who's he?"

"Mr. Codsworth is a big inflatable fish tied to a branch next to the lake," April said. "The first canoe to reach Mr. Codsworth and bring him back to camp wins the first gold star for their cabin."

April explained how each time a cabin wins a challenge, the Clancys hang a gold star on the group's door. At the end of the summer the cabin with the most gold stars is named Cabin of the Year.

"Did you hear that?" Vicky gasped. She turned to Ashley, Kimberly, and me. "We can be the best cabin at Camp Crooked Lake!"

April shook her head. "I didn't say the best—"

"I did!" Vicky interrupted. "I have the best clothes! The best sleepovers! The best toys and games on the block! Why shouldn't I have the best cabin?"

Wow! I thought. *Vicki is* way *competitive!*

We were halfway down the trail when a group of boy campers caught up with us. April introduced us to their senior counselor. "This is Dave. He is in charge of Robin Cabin."

"Hi," Dave said with a smile.

A boy with a spiky haircut and a chipped tooth stepped forward. The name scrawled on his duffel bag was Dexter.

"Robins rule!" Dexter said.

Vicki stared straight into his eyes. "I don't think so," she said. "*Blackbirds* rule...Robins drool!"

Dexter shook his head and ran back to his friends. We continued along the trail to our cabin. On the way we passed Sparrow Cabin and Eagle Cabin. *I wonder how much farther it is to Blackbird Cabin*, I thought.

I turned to ask April, but she and Dave were walking in back of the group, whispering to each other.

What are they talking about? I wondered. I slowed down so I could hear them.

"Did you tell the campers about the curse yet?" April asked.

"No way," Dave said. "I don't want to scare them. They just got here."

Uh-oh.

Did I hear right?

Did April say a curse?

Hmmm. Maybe Ashley and I were going to have a case to solve at summer camp after all!

2

A NEW MYSTERY

I listened to April and Dave talk some more, but they didn't say another word about a curse.

I raced to catch up with Ashley. "I just heard the weirdest thing." I told her what April and Dave had said.

Ashley smiled and shook her head. "They were probably just planning a scary story for around the campfire!" she said.

I glanced over my shoulder. Dave was starting to lead his group down another trail.

"You must be right," I said, smiling, too. "What would a campfire be without scary stories?"

"That cabin up ahead is ours," April called out.

"Excellent! Come on, Mary-Kate!" Ashley pulled me toward the wooden building.

Blackbird Cabin was the coolest. Inside there were two sets of bunk beds and four built-in chests for our clothes.

"Why don't you guys unpack? I'll see you at the lake in half an hour," April said. She waved and left.

"This is a great cabin," Kimberly said.

"Are you serious?" Vicki scoffed. "My room at home is bigger than this!" She unzipped her duffel bag and stuffed some of her clothes into one of the chests.

"I think it's just right." I grabbed my sleeping bag and tossed it onto one of the bottom bunks.

"Hey, that's the bed I was going to take,"

Vicki whined. "It's right by the window with the best view."

"Okay." I shrugged. "You can sleep here if you really want." I moved my sleeping bag to the other bottom bunk.

Wham! The cabin door flew open. A girl with frizzy brown hair and a Camp Crooked Lake T-shirt ran inside.

"Whew!" she said. "I didn't think it would take this long to get back from the storage shed. I'm Joy, your junior counselor."

"I'm Mary-Kate Olsen," I said.

"Nice to meet you, Mary-Kate." Joy stuck out her hand for me to shake.

I touched Joy's palm. A sharp tingle ran through my fingers and way up my arm. "Yee-ow!" I cried. "Make it stop!"

"Gotcha!" Joy cried. She let go of my hand. The tingling feeling disappeared.

Joy showed me her palm. Lying on it was a small metal circle. "Surprise!" She laughed.

"It's a hand buzzer!" Ashley said.

"Right." Joy grinned. "When you squeeze it, it gives you a shock. Want to try it again?"

"Um—no, thanks," I said quickly.

"I just *love* playing jokes on people," Joy told us.

"Uh-oh." Kimberly giggled. "We'd better check our chairs for whoopee cushions!"

"That's right." Joy wiggled her eyebrows at us. "You never know where I'll strike next!"

We all giggled. Joy seemed like lots of fun.

"Put on shorts and T-shirts, everyone," Joy instructed. "Then I'll take you down to the lake for the canoe race."

We all changed as fast as we could and walked down to the lake.

"Hey, Blackbirds!" Vicki called out. She held up her hand for high-fives. "We're going to win this race! After all, my name is

Vicki—and that's short for *Victory*!"

After high-fiving us, Vicki ran ahead.

When we reached the lake, April was there to meet us. The other campers were starting to arrive with their counselors, too.

While we waited for the canoe instruction to start, Ashley and I tossed around a purple Frisbee.

"Got it!" I called. I ran and jumped into the air to catch it. When I landed, I was standing next to the four senior counselors.

"When should we tell them about the curse?" Mike asked.

"Shh!" Sandi whispered. "Not yet. We'll tell them later."

Whoa! I thought. *They're not talking about a campfire story. There* is *some kind of curse at Camp Crooked Lake!*

I ran over to Ashley. "I heard it again!" I told her. "Mike and Sandi were definitely talking about a curse!"

"Mary-Kate!" Ashley grinned. "I think

you've been solving too many mysteries lately. I'm sure it's part of the campfire story."

Ashley grabbed my arm. "Mike just blew his whistle. He wants us to line up on the shore with our counselors."

"The first step," Mike began, "is to take a life vest and try it on for size."

April and Joy showed us how to strap on the bright orange life vests. Then we were each given an aluminum oar.

"What are we waiting for?" Vicki asked. She pointed her oar to the rows of silver canoes in the water. "Let's go for the gold. Stars, that is!"

"Not until you learn how to paddle first," April said.

With the help of the counselors, we practiced the forward stroke, backstroke, and something called a J-stroke.

When we all got the hang of it, it was time to board our shiny silver canoes. I sat in the bow, Ashley took the stern, and Vicki and Kimberly sat in the middle.

We giggled as the canoe began to wobble.

"Remember, campers!" Mike called as we paddled our canoe to the starting line. "The red ribbons on the trees will lead you straight to Mr. Codsworth. The blue ones will lead you back to camp."

"The lake gets really twisty," Dave added. "So get ready to rock and roll!"

Tweeeeeet! Mike blew his whistle again, and we were off! I held the oar at the top and the middle and stroked it forward. But instead of going ahead, we swerved to the right.

"Vicki!" I called over my shoulder. "We're all supposed to stroke at the same time."

"Just paddle faster!" Vicki shouted. "We need speed!"

The lake did get twisty as we paddled on. The Raven Cabin's canoe got stuck in the brush and mud. The Bluebirds' boat began to lag behind. But we were way up front!

"Heads up, Blackbirds," Ashley called from the back. "The Robin boys are right behind us."

"The *Robin* boys?" Vicki gasped.

I looked over my shoulder and saw the Robins paddling nearby. Dexter was at the bow, just like me.

"Bye-bye, Blackbirds!" Dexter sneered. "Robins are gonna fly!"

"Watch this!" Vicki whispered. She whacked the water with her oar. A big wave hit the Robins' canoe.

"Hey!" Dexter shouted.

"Quit it!" a boy wearing glasses complained.

I shook my head. Vicki would do anything to win—even if it meant being nasty!

We paddled harder. After a few minutes we were leading the race by a mile! Then up ahead I saw it—a rubber fish tied to an overhanging branch. The fish bounced in the water.

"It's him!" I shouted. "Mr. Codsworth!"

"Ye-es!" Vicki cheered. The canoe rocked as she pumped her fist in the air. "I told you we were the best!"

We glided our canoe straight over to Mr. Codsworth. I reached over and struggled to untie him.

"Try getting out and doing it," Ashley advised.

Carefully I stepped out of the canoe onto the muddy bank of the lake. I untied Mr. Codsworth and tossed him to Ashley.

I was just about to jump back into our boat when I noticed something colorful and shiny hanging from a nearby tree.

It looked like a cool beaded necklace. I ran to the tree and plucked it off the branch.

How pretty! I thought as I slipped the necklace over my head. The beads were turquoise, orange, and brown. A silver medallion shaped like a crescent moon dangled at the end.

I'll bring this back to camp, I thought. *Just in case someone lost it.*

I ran back to the canoe, jumped in, and grabbed my paddle.

"Neat necklace!" Kimberly said. "I love half-moons."

"I like *stars* better!" Vicki declared. She dug her oar into the water. "Gold stars, if you know what I mean!"

As we paddled back to camp with Mr. Codsworth, the counselors cheered.

"Way to go, Blackbirds!" April shouted as we rowed in. She helped us drag our canoe onto the shore.

"Where's Joy?" Kimberly asked.

"She said she wanted to take a walk," April said. "Too bad she missed your big win!"

I picked up Mr. Codsworth and held him

high. "Ta-daaaa!" I declared. "The catch of the day!"

I tossed Mr. Codsworth to April. Then I lifted the necklace from my throat.

"Look what else I found," I said. "It was in a tree right near Mr. Codsworth. Do you think it belongs to anybody, April?"

April gasped. Her eyes popped wide open. She dropped Mr. Codsworth on the sand and stared at the necklace.

"Th-that necklace!" she stammered. "It can't be!"

I glanced at the other counselors. Their mouths hung open. They all seemed scared, too!

"What is it?" I asked.

April peered closer at the necklace. Then she slowly backed away from me.

"The legend is true!" she declared. "There really is a curse on Camp Crooked Lake—and Mary-Kate has awakened it!"

3

THE CURSE OF
CAMP CROOKED LAKE

"**C**urse?" I looked at Ashley and then at the counselors. "You mean the curse you were talking about before?"

By now all of the campers had rowed to shore. Everyone crowded around April.

"Anyone who has been here before knows this story," April said. "We tell it around the campfire every year, but none of us ever thought it was true." She took a deep breath. "The land surrounding this lake used to belong to an Indian tribe. But hundreds of years ago, English settlers drove the Indians away...."

Dave picked up the story. "Before the Indians left, they put a curse on the lake. Anyone who awakened the curse would be driven off this land by magical forces."

A huge lump formed in my throat. I didn't like where this was going!

"But how does the curse work?" Kimberly asked.

"Legend says that the Indians hung a special necklace near the lake," April explained. "And anyone who took the necklace would awaken the curse."

Like me, I thought, swallowing hard.

"But no one ever found a necklace," Sandi said. "So we thought the curse was just a silly legend."

Dave groaned. "Until now!"

My knees felt like jelly. "Does this mean—*I'm* cursed?" I asked.

"According to the legend," April said,

"once the curse is awakened, anyone on this land is cursed. That means the whole camp is doomed!"

"The whole camp?" a Raven boy cried.

"Oh, no!" a Bluebird girl wailed.

"You just had to take that stupid necklace, Mary-Kate!" Vicki said angrily.

My mouth was too dry to speak. But Ashley came to my rescue.

"Oh, curse-shmurse!" Ashley told Vicki. "I don't believe in curses. And neither does Mary-Kate."

"Right!" I said. I took the necklace off and tossed it to Dave.

Dave caught the necklace as though it were red hot. "Maybe if I get rid of this, the curse will be reversed." His voice shook. "But I doubt it!"

"So what do we do now?" Kimberly asked.

April shook her head. "I don't know." She sighed. "I just don't know!"

4

COOKOUT CAPER

"What do you like to put on your hot dogs, Kimberly?" I asked. "Ketchup, mustard, or relish?"

Kimberly grinned. It was a half an hour before the first cookout. So far, nothing bad had happened because of the curse, so everyone was feeling a little better.

We Blackbirds were hanging out inside our cabin. April had gone to a senior counselor meeting. Joy was writing postcards on her bed.

"I like my hot dogs plain," Kimberly said.

"*Naked* hot dogs?" Vicki scoffed. "Boring!" She sat down on her bed to tie her sneaker. We all heard a loud—BLUUUUR-RRRP!

Vicki's face turned red. She reached under her mattress and pulled out a whoopee cushion.

"Gotcha!" Joy called from her bed. She laughed so hard, she almost dropped the postcard she was writing.

Ashley, Kimberly, and I giggled, too. The only one *not* laughing was Vicki!

"Very funny!" she snapped.

"I thought so!" Joy said. Then she jumped off her bunk. "Whoops. I almost forgot. Who wants to help me pick up the food and coolers and bring them down to the lake for the pigout? I mean—cookout."

"I will!" I said, raising my hand.

"Mary-Kate!" Vicki called as we left the cabin. "Don't pick up any more necklaces!"

I frowned. "Thanks for the tip," I muttered.

Joy and I walked up to the main lodge. The lodge was huge. It was old-fashioned-looking, and it was made of big stones and logs.

"This lodge has been here for a long time," Joy told me. "I think some settlers lived here many years back."

"Neat," I said, stepping into the dining hall.

"Check it out." Joy pointed to an enormous bear rug hanging from the wall.

"Yikes!" I said. "Look at those huge claws!"

"I wouldn't want to run into him in the woods," Joy admitted.

"We won't see any bears out there tonight, right?" I asked.

"No way. I already asked," Joy said. "No one has seen a bear around here for ten years."

Whew. I breathed a sigh of relief.

We pushed through a swinging door and entered the kitchen. There were two big, empty coolers on the floor.

I found the hot dogs and buns and tossed them into one of the coolers. Joy tossed bags of marshmallows and squeeze bottles of ketchup and mustard into the other one.

"We'll have to come back for the soda," Joy told me.

"Don't bother," a voice said.

I turned and saw Mr. Clancy standing in the doorway. His eyes were cold as ice and his mouth formed a grim line.

"Excuse me?" I asked in a squeaky voice.

"Don't bother coming back for the bottles," Mr. Clancy said. "If you give me a few minutes, I'll bring them down to the cookout myself."

"Thanks, Mr. C.!" Joy said.

Mr. Clancy nodded and went into a small

office attached to the kitchen. He was still frowning.

He is definitely not happy to be at camp, I thought.

"Mary-Kate," Joy said, "why don't you take one cooler and I'll take the other?"

"Sure," I replied.

Joy and I lifted the coolers and brought them down to the lake. The campers cheered as we placed them on a wooden picnic table. The table was covered with a white paper tablecloth.

"Come and get it!" Joy called.

"Not so fast, campers!" Dave called back. "First we have to learn the Camp Crooked Lake song. Then we eat!"

Joy arranged the coolers on the picnic table as we all gathered around Dave and his guitar. He began strumming and reciting the lyrics.

"'When the yellow sun rises,'" he sang, "'each morning we wake, and have a good time down at Camp Crooked Lake! Camp Crooked Lake! Camp Crooked Lake! No, there's nothing twisted 'bout Camp Crooked Lake!'"

I was about to sing the first round, when I saw the boys from Robin Cabin. They were scurrying up the path that led to the cabins.

What are they up to? I wondered.

After singing a full round, it was finally time to eat. All the campers raced over to the picnic table. The bottles of soda were there. But when the counselors lifted the lids from the coolers—

"Hey!" I cried. "Our food is gone!"

THE CURSE STRIKES!

I stared inside both coolers. I couldn't believe it. They *were* empty. No hot dogs, marshmallows, buns—nothing!

"Didn't you and Mary-Kate fill the coolers, Joy?" April asked.

"We sure did," Joy insisted.

"Then where's the food?" April asked.

"I don't know." Joy shook her head. "It's as if it just disappeared...." Her voice trailed off.

"It's because of the curse!" Vicki declared.

I glanced around. All eyes were suddenly on me!

"Oh, come on, Vicki," Ashley said. "The woods are full of little creatures. Maybe a raccoon ate the cookout food."

"A raccoon? Did he put the cooler lids back on when he finished?" Vicki laughed. "I don't think so. And besides, only a ten-foot-tall raccoon could eat all that food!"

"A ten-foot-tall raccoon?" One of the youngest campers wailed. "I don't like it here! I want to go home!"

My eyes darted back to the table. Our tablecloth was gone, too. What was going on?

Mike forced a big smile. "Uh—come on, you guys!" he said. "There must be some logical explanation."

"Right," Joy agreed. "And who says we have to eat hot dogs? There's plenty of peanut butter and jelly in the kitchen!"

"Peanut butter?" Vicki cried. "At a cookout?"

"That's a great idea!" April said. "And I think there's some chocolate pudding in the fridge for dessert."

"Terrific!" Joy jumped up from her seat. "I'll go get it."

Everyone sat silently, waiting for Joy to return. I was about to say something to Ashley, when I felt a weird tickle up my leg. I glanced down and saw a little black ant.

I shook my leg to get the ant off. But then another ant scurried up my arm! I brushed it away, and saw another ant crawl over my knee! Then another creeped between my fingers!

"Mary-Kate!" Ashley cried. "There's an army of ants marching up my leg!"

I looked around and saw that everyone else was wiggling, swatting, and stomping, too!

"It's an ant invasion!" Vicki shrieked. "Run!"

The campers raced for the rec hall. The

counselors followed close behind.

"I don't understand it!" Ashley said once we were indoors. "Ants are usually drawn to food. But we didn't have any food at the cookout."

"It's the curse," Vicki insisted loudly. "The ants were sent by the angry spirits to drive us off the land! And it's all Mary-Kate's fault!"

I found a quiet table in the rec hall and took a seat.

Ashley grabbed two peanut-butter-and-jelly sandwiches from April. She sat down next to me and handed me a sandwich.

"Thanks," I mumbled.

"Hey, what's wrong?" Ashley asked.

"What's *wrong*?" I stared at her wide-eyed. "Everything's wrong! Everyone thinks there's a curse on this camp! And I'm starting to believe they're right!"

Ashley frowned. "Come on. We both know there is no such thing as a curse."

"Hey, everyone. Listen up!" Dave said. "We're going to take a moonlight hike around the lake. So when you're finished eating, grab your sweatshirts from your cabins and we'll meet back here."

Ashley and I finished our sandwiches quickly and headed back to our cabin.

While Ashley found her sweatshirt, I sat down on my bed.

"I think I got a pebble in my sneaker," I said.

"Mary-Kate, get up!" Ashley cried as I reached for my sneaker. "Now!"

"Why?" I asked, jumping off the bed.

"Look." Ashley pointed behind me.

I turned and glanced at my bunk. Something was curled on top of my sleeping bag. Something long and slithering.

"A snake!" I screamed. "Help! There's a snake in my bed!"

6

S-S-SNEAK ATTACK

"**D**on't shout!" Ashley said. "If you scare the snakes, they might slither off and hide. Then we'll never find them."

"*Them?*" I squeaked.

Ashley pointed to Vicki's bunk. "There's another one."

I gasped. Ashley was right. A second greenish-brown snake was curled up on Vicki's bed!

Ashley climbed onto one of the cubby chests. She peered onto her bunk. "There's one on my bed, too!" she whispered. She turned her head. "And on Kimberly's!"

SLAM! The door flew open and Vicki and Kimberly stepped into the cabin. Joy and April followed behind them.

"We heard you yelling. Are you okay?" Kimberly asked.

Vicki screamed before I could answer. "Snakes!" she shrieked. "There are snakes in here!"

Vicki was so loud, the snake on her bed started to uncurl. She screamed again and leaped away.

I heard more yelling outside. I peeked out the window and saw campers running in and out of their cabins.

"Snakes!" the other campers yelled. "Help! Snakes!"

"Whoa!" I shook my head. "Everyone has snakes in their cabins!"

"Calm down," April said. "Those are just garden snakes. They're totally harmless."

"I'll take them out in the woods and let them go," Joy said. She quickly picked up all four snakes. They wriggled in her hands as she headed for the door. "Then I'll give the other cabins a hand."

I stared at Joy as she left the cabin. She didn't seem afraid of the snakes at all.

"Make sure you take them *way* out!" Vicki called after Joy. Then she glared at me. "Thanks again, Mary-Kate!"

"Mary-Kate didn't put the snakes in the cabins!" Ashley protested.

"Yes, she did," Vicki said. "She brought the curse and the curse brought the snakes!"

"This *is* getting a little scary," Kimberly admitted.

Vicki stormed out of the cabin. Kimberly and April left to see how the other campers were doing.

"Ashley," I said slowly after everyone was gone, "that's the fourth scary thing that's happened to us today. What if there really *is* a curse?"

"I told you, there is no such thing as a curse," Ashley said. "Anyone could have put the snakes in the cabins while we were out." She grabbed her pencil and notebook from her backpack.

"What are you doing?" I asked.

"It's time to make a list of suspects," Ashley said. "We have a mystery to solve!"

She opened her notebook to the first blank page. "Who would want to make it look like there's a curse on Camp Crooked Lake?" she asked.

I frowned. "Scaring people with a fake curse seems like a really mean joke," I said. "And there's one person here who really likes jokes—Joy. Could she be a suspect?"

"She went for a walk during our canoe race," Ashley pointed out. "She could have planted the necklace while we were all rowing."

"And I left her near the picnic table with the food. She could have stashed it somewhere when everyone else wasn't looking!" I said.

"What about the snakes?" Ashley asked.

"Joy had no problem carrying the snakes *out* of the cabins," I said. "Maybe she put them *in* everyone's cabin, too."

Ashley agreed. She wrote Suspect #1: Joy, in her detective pad.

"Who else might want everyone to think there is a curse?" she asked.

We thought as hard as we could, but neither of us could come up with a single person.

Ashley sighed. "It looks like Joy is our only suspect for now," she said. "Let's go out and see if the hike is still on."

"And let's keep an eye on Joy," I added.

On our way back to the rec hall, we passed the main lodge. Through an open window I saw Mr. and Mrs. Clancy in the dining room.

"We've been running this camp for over twenty years!" we heard Mr. Clancy shout. "It's time to close up!"

"Absolutely not," Mrs. Clancy insisted.

Ashley and I exchanged puzzled looks. We stopped to listen more closely.

"I'm tired of working so hard," Mr. Clancy said. "I'm tired of bug spray and baked beans. I want to retire!"

"We have had this discussion a hundred times," Mrs. Clancy reminded him. "And my feelings haven't changed. We are not closing the camp."

"We'll just see about that," Mr. Clancy muttered.

I turned to Ashley. "So, *that's* why Mr. Clancy is so grouchy," I whispered. "He wants to close the camp!"

"I think we just found Suspect Number Two!" Ashley said. "If the campers think there's a curse here, no one will want to come back. And if there are no campers, then there is no camp," she finished.

"Mr. Clancy could have put the necklace in the woods," I pointed out. "And he could have put the snakes in everyone's bunks."

"And while we were having our sing-along, Mr. Clancy brought the bottles of soda to the picnic table," Ashley said. "He could have taken the food then!"

"Plus, when he brought the bottles of soda," I added, "he could have also brought some jars—of *ants*!"

Ashley quickly wrote Suspect #2, Mr. Clancy in her pad. "Now we have two suspects," Ashley said.

"Tomorrow we will have to do some major snooping," I told her. "I want to solve this mystery before the curse strikes again!"

7

FOOD FOR THOUGHT

"I hardly slept a wink last night," Ashley whispered to me the next morning. "I kept thinking about the case."

"Oh, yeah?" I asked. "*I* kept thinking there were more snakes in my bed."

I poured myself a cup of orange juice. The Blackbirds were seated at a large table for breakfast. April and Joy were busy passing out plates of scrambled eggs.

"No bacon for me," Vicki said. "I don't want anything on my plate that looks like a snake!"

I tried to ignore Vicki. I was about take a sip of my juice, when Kimberly jumped up in her seat.

"Oh, no!" she cried.

"What is it?" April asked.

Kimberly pointed to her paper cup. "There's something floating in my juice!"

I peered into Kimberly's cup and gasped. An eyeball was bobbing around inside!

"Gotcha again!" Joy snickered. She reached into Kimberly's juice and pulled out the eyeball. "These rubber eyes look just like the real thing, don't you think?"

Ashley and I exchanged a glance. Suspect #1 sure did like scaring people.

"Okay." April sighed. "Everybody just settle down and eat breakfast."

I took a forkful of scrambled eggs. Ashley jabbed my arm with her elbow.

"What?" I asked.

Ashley nodded toward the next table. The boys from the Robin Cabin were just sitting down. "Check out their sneakers," Ashley whispered. "They're caked with red and yellow stuff!"

"So?" I asked.

"So," Ashley said, "someone swiped the food last night—including some bottles of ketchup and mustard. What color is ketchup and mustard?"

"Yellow and red," I said slowly.

A boy named Jack caught us staring at his sneakers. "What are you looking at?" he called over.

"Nothing." Ashley shrugged.

"I spotted the Robins sneaking away from the cookout right before the food disappeared," I whispered. "Maybe we should put them on our suspect list."

"Maybe." Ashley thought for a second. "But how could the Robins have placed that necklace in the woods? They arrived at camp when we did. Then they were in the canoe race. They didn't have time."

"You're right," I said. "But something tells me Dexter and his bunkmates are up to something."

"Hey! Where is Dexter?" Ashley asked. "He's not at the table."

"Maybe he's pigging out on the food he took last night," I suggested. "Come on. Let's check out Robin Cabin!"

"What if we run into Dexter?" Ashley asked.

"Then we question him!" I said. I turned to our senior counselor. "April? Is it okay if Ashley and I run back to our cabin? We forgot…we forgot…"

"Our vitamins!" Ashley chimed in.

"Okay," April told us. "Go ahead."

"Thanks!" Ashley and I bolted out of the dining room.

"Look!" Ashley said when we reached the doorstep to Robin Cabin.

I glanced down and saw a glob of red goo on the floor. Could it be ketchup?

Ashley grabbed the handle on the door. It squeaked as she slowly opened it. "Now, remember," she whispered as we stepped inside the cabin. "Be on the lookout for hot dogs, marshmallows, ketchup, mustard—"

"And stinky socks!" I joked, pointing to a pile of dirty laundry.

We found more red and yellow splats on the floor. Then—

"Hey!" Ashley whispered. She pointed over my shoulder.

I spun around. Dexter was inching his way toward the back door. He was carrying a white bundle—white as in *white table-cloth*!

"Get him!" I cried.

8

THE ROBIN'S SECRET

Ashley and I chased Dexter out the door and through the campgrounds.

"Get lost!" Dexter hollered as he ran. He was fast—but the white cloth he was carrying began to unroll. He stumbled over it and fell to the ground.

I ran up to Dexter and grabbed the cloth. Then I whipped it open. But what I found inside wasn't food. It was a picture of a red robin splashed across a yellow background!

"Rats!" Dexter grumbled. "You weren't

supposed to see that until we hung it on our cabin door."

"What is it?" I asked.

"Duh! It's a banner!" Dexter said, still on the ground. "We painted it late last night while our counselors were at the canteen."

"*Paint?*" Ashley repeated. "You mean this isn't ketchup and mustard?"

"What are you talking about?" Dexter asked as he stood up. "We borrowed the paint from the arts and crafts hut."

I took a whiff of the cloth. It *was* paint!

"But this is the tablecloth from the cookout last night," Ashley said. "Isn't it?"

Dexter dug the tip of his sneaker into the dirt. "Yeah." He nodded. "We needed it for the banner."

Oh, I thought. Dexter and the Robins didn't steal the food. Just the tablecloth!

"Okay, campers, join your cabin groups!" Dave shouted late that afternoon. "It's almost time to leave for the camp-out."

We gathered near the trails in front of the lodge. We were getting ready to hike into the woods and camp there overnight.

"Did anyone see Joy?" April asked.

"The last time I saw her was before lunch," Vicki said.

"Well, we can't leave without her," April said. "While you're waiting, check your backpacks one more time. Make sure you have everything you need."

I unzipped my pack. "Joy is missing again," I said to Ashley. "What do you think she's up to?"

"Maybe she's setting up another surprise," Ashley answered. "One that everyone will blame on the curse!" She glanced up. "Hey, look! There's Mr. Clancy."

I turned my head toward the lodge. Mr. Clancy was coming out the side door. He had something big and bulky in his arms.

"What is he carrying?" I asked.

"There's only one way to find out," Ashley said. "Let's follow him!"

Ashley and I took two steps toward Mr. Clancy. Then—

"Hi, everyone! Sorry I'm late!" Joy said, running up to us. "I took a walk and lost track of time."

I raised my eyebrows at Ashley. Did Joy lose track of time—while she was planning another trick?

"Hey, does anybody want some gum?" Joy asked. She pulled a pack from her jeans pocket.

"I'll take some," Ashley said. She put a piece in her mouth and started chewing. Suddenly her face turned red. Her eyes grew wide.

"Mmmph!" Ashley spit the gum into its wrapper. "It's hot and spicy!" she cried.

Joy burst out laughing. "Gotcha!" she yelled. "It's trick gum. It's supposed to taste nasty. You should have seen your face just now, Ashley. It was hilarious!"

"Somebody should play a trick on Joy and see how *she* likes it," Ashley whispered to me.

Tweeeeet! The senior counselors blew their whistles.

"Listen up!" Mike called. "Each cabin group will hike on a different trail to the campsite. Your junior counselors will lead you."

"What about the senior counselors?" Kimberly asked.

"We're bringing the tents and the food and supplies on a separate trail," Sandi replied. "We'll meet up with you later."

"Follow me, Blackbirds!" Joy said. She started along the winding trail.

As we hiked, Kimberly pointed out all the different kinds of birds and plants along our path.

"You sure know a lot about nature," Ashley said.

"I belong to the Outdoor Club at school," Kimberly said. "We go hiking every weekend."

"I'm tired," Vicki complained. "Are we there yet?"

"I don't think we have that much farther to go," Joy answered. "See where the path divides up ahead?"

I nodded. "It splits in three different directions. Which way do we go?"

"We take the trail to the right," Joy said. "Come on, everyone, let's go!"

"Everyone's walking too slowly," Vicki complained. "I'll meet you guys at the campsite." She ran down the trail.

"Vicki, wait!" Joy shouted. "You don't know where you're going."

"I'll be fine," Vicki called back.

"I'm supposed to keep the group together," Joy told us. "Everyone follow me!"

We ran down the trail after Vicki. It twisted farther into the deep, dark woods.

At the end of the trail we found Vicki, plus the Bluebirds, the Ravens, the Eagles, the Robins, and the Sparrows. They stood frozen like statues in front of a giant boulder.

"Hey, you guys," I said as we approached the group. "What's going on? Why are you all just standing here?"

"Look." With a shaky finger Dexter pointed to the boulder.

I turned and saw a message scrawled across the rock. A shiver ran up my spine as I read the words. "Beware the Curse of Crooked Lake!"

"It's a warning!" Vicki cried. "A warning from the Indian tribe that cursed the lake!"

Ashley peered at the writing. She touched it, then rubbed her fingers together. "This message is written in chalk. Anybody could have put it here."

"So what?" Vicki cried. "It's still a warning. The spirits want us off their land!"

"Quiet down," the Eagles' junior counselor said. "The first thing we need to do is find the senior counselors. So let's move."

The campers followed the junior counselors down another trail. Ashley and I stayed behind for a minute.

"Think, Mary-Kate," Ashley said. "Which of our suspects could have written this message?"

"Joy was late starting the hike," I said. "She could have sneaked into the woods and written that message."

"And don't forget Mr. Clancy," Ashley pointed out. "After twenty-five years he must know these woods inside out. He could have written the message, too!"

I nodded. "So we still can't rule out any suspects!"

"What we need are clues," Ashley said. "Keep your eyes peeled, Mary-Kate!"

We hurried to catch up with the others. With each step we took, the woods seemed to grow darker.

We turned onto another trail—and heard the faint sound of a harmonica.

"There's someone up ahead!" Kimberly exclaimed.

We ran around a bend in the trail and saw the campsite—and our senior counselors. Dave put down his harmonica when he saw us. "There you are!" he said. "What took you so long?"

"We found a message on a boulder," Vicki told him. "It said to beware the curse of Crooked Lake!"

"Really?" April asked nervously.

"Really." Vicki nodded. She folded her arms over her chest. "There is no way I'm staying in these woods tonight. I want to go back to the cabin—right *now!*"

"Well…okay," April said. "Mr. and Mrs. Clancy are back at camp. You can stay with them. If you really want to go, Joy can take you there."

"But how do I get back?" Joy asked.

"We're not very far from the lodge now," Mike said. He pointed to some nearby trees. "Right behind those trees is the path that we took to the campsite. It leads directly to camp."

"You just had to take that dumb necklace, didn't you, Mary-Kate?" Vicki said. "You had to ruin our whole summer."

After our tents were set up, the group sang songs around the campfire. Dave played his guitar. Then we feasted on chili and s'mores. By the time we went to bed, the campers were in pretty good spirits.

Ashley and I crawled into our tent. I closed my eyes and started to drift off to sleep.

"Mary-Kate." Ashley tapped me on the shoulder. "Didn't you eat enough at dinner?"

"Sure," I answered her. "Why?"

"Because your stomach is growling," she replied.

"No, it's not," I said.

"Well, *something* is growling!" Ashley insisted.

We sat up and heard a rustling sound in the woods.

"What's that?" we heard Kimberly ask in the tent next to ours.

Ashley and I scrambled outside. So did everyone else.

Crrrack! Crrrack! Snap! Something huge and heavy was crashing through the woods. But what?

I squinted, trying to see through the thick cover of the trees.

There! A dark figure was moving toward our campsite.

I caught a glimpse of fur!

Then the figure turned toward me.

I saw claws! And eyes! And giant teeth!

"It's a bear!" I shouted.

9

GRIN AND BEAR IT

"**D**on't panic!" Dave shouted.

Too late. Everyone screamed their heads off.

The bear lurched forward and we screamed again.

I held my breath as the bear stared at us. He stared and stared. Then he turned and moved off into the woods.

"Let's all head back to our cabins right now!" Mike suggested. "We can pick up our stuff tomorrow."

Everyone agreed. The counselors flicked on their flashlights, and we headed for camp.

At breakfast the next morning, I noticed that the other campers were avoiding me. "They're afraid of the curse!" I whispered to Ashley. "And I don't blame them. Even *we* can't explain the bear."

"There's got to be a logical answer," Ashley said. "We just have to keep searching for it."

We stopped at a long table filled with muffins, rolls, and juice. I was about to grab a blueberry muffin when I glanced up at the bear rug.

Something about it looked...strange.

"Ashley," I said, wrinkling my nose. "What's all that stuff sticking to the rug?"

Ashley peered up. "It's twigs!" she said. "See? The fur has little twigs and pieces of leaves stuck in it."

Twigs? Leaves? How could they have gotten on the rug? Unless...

"Ashley, that rug was clean yesterday!" I exclaimed. "Do you think somebody wore that rug in the woods last night to scare us?"

"Maybe," Ashley said. "Remember who we saw yesterday before we left on the camp-out?"

"Mr. Clancy!" I answered. "*And* he was carrying something out of the lodge."

"I bet it was the bear rug!" Ashley said. "Let's go back to the campsite and search for clues."

"Okay," I agreed. "Maybe Mr. Clancy left something behind."

We scarfed down our muffins and ran back to the campsite. The counselors were going to pick up the tents and backpacks soon, so we had to hurry.

"I'm going to check the branches for little pieces of material," Ashley said. "Whoever took the rug might have snagged their clothes."

"I'll check the ground," I said. "Maybe Mr. Clancy dropped something." I walked to the exact spot where I had seen the bear. At first, all I found were pine needles. But then—

"Shoeprints!" I cried. "Ashley, look!"

Ashley and I examined the shoeprints. "The soles have a diamond pattern on them," I pointed out. "If Mr. Clancy's shoes have diamond patterns on them, too, this case is closed!"

Ashley put her foot next to one of the prints. "Wait a minute, Mary-Kate. These prints are about the same size as mine. Mr. Clancy is much bigger than I am. There's no way these could be his footprints."

I frowned. I felt sure that Mr. Clancy was our culprit. But Ashley was right. Mr. Clancy's feet were way bigger than ours were.

"What about Joy?" Ashley asked. "She's

still on our suspect list. Could these prints be hers?"

"Why not?" I said. "Joy went back to the cabins with Vicki. She could have grabbed the rug after that and sneaked over here to scare us."

"Let's go talk to her," I suggested.

We headed down the path toward camp—and heard someone humming in the woods ahead of us.

"Who is that?" I asked.

Ashley peered through the trees. "It's Joy!" She pointed toward a hiker on the trail next to ours.

"Let's follow her," I said. "She might be planning another nasty trick. Maybe we can catch her in the act!"

Joy was moving super-fast, so we picked up our pace. We sneaked along behind her, careful not to make a sound.

Then she stopped—and glanced over her shoulder!

Ashley and I dived behind a big bush.

"Oof!" I said as I fell into a branch. "Did she see us?"

Ashley and I held our breath. After a few seconds, I peeked out from behind the bush.

Joy was standing right there, staring at us. She had her hands on her hips, and she looked mad!

"Just what do you think you're doing?" she asked.

"Uh-oh," I muttered to Ashley. "We're toast."

10

CAUGHT SNOOPING

"I *thought* I saw you two following me!" Joy exclaimed. "What's going on?"

"That's what we want to ask," Ashley replied. "What are *you* up to?"

"Up to?" Joy repeated. "Why would you think I'm up to something?"

"Because of all your practical jokes," I said. "Especially the bear one."

Joy looked confused. "What are you talking about?" she asked.

"We saw leaves and twigs in the bear rug

at the lodge this morning," Ashley said.

"And we found someone's footprints in the woods," I added. "That means somebody took the bear rug from the lodge last night and scared us with it. Somebody who is trying to make everyone believe in the curse of Camp Crooked Lake."

"Well, it wasn't me!" Joy insisted. "I didn't go near that rug."

I stared at the ground near Joy's feet. Her short hiking boots had left prints in the dirt. Prints that looked like swirls. Not diamonds.

"Do you have any other shoes here at camp?" I asked.

Joy shook her head. "No. All I have are my hiking boots."

"How do we know you're telling the truth?" I asked.

Joy held up her hands. "Look—I didn't dress like a bear. And I'm not trying to make anyone believe in the curse. Honest. The only pranks I pulled were the gum, the floating eyeball, the whoopee cushion, and the hand buzzer!"

"But you were missing during the canoe race—right before we found the Indian necklace. And you were late for the hike yesterday—right before we found that creepy message on the rock," I pointed out.

"So if you weren't planting the necklace or writing that message, where were you?" Ashley asked.

Joy sighed. "My best friend, Sally, is a junior counselor at Camp Lookout." She pointed behind her down the trail. "It's about a ten-minute walk from here. When we figured out how close we were, we made plans to meet up once in a while. That's why I wasn't at the canoe race. And that's why I was late for the hike yesterday."

Ashley and I glanced at each other.

"I'm going to see Sally right now," Joy told us. "If you don't believe me, come and ask her yourself."

"Okay," I agreed. "We will."

Joy hurried down the trail. Ashley and I ran after her. Soon we came to a big flat rock. A girl wearing a red Camp Lookout T-shirt was sitting on top of it.

The girl turned toward us.

We saw a long pointy arrow sticking right through her head!

Ashley and I gasped.

"Hi!" the girl said. "I guess I got a little too close to archcry practice.... Ouch!"

The girl pulled the arrow off her head like a headband. "Gotcha!" she said.

I sighed with relief. It was one of those goofy trick arrows. And it sure tricked us!

"Good one, Sally!" Joy laughed. "I've got to remember that."

"Thanks!" Sally smiled.

"This is Mary-Kate and Ashley," Joy introduced us. "They're two of my campers. They want to ask you something."

"Ask away!" Sally said.

"Mary-Kate and I need to know the last time that you and Joy met," Ashley told her.

Sally frowned. "I think it was…yesterday afternoon," she said. "Late afternoon."

Hmmm. That was just before we started our hike to the overnight campsite, I realized.

"What about the time before that?" I asked.

Sally's eyebrows knitted together. "I guess it was two days ago," she told us. "Around noon."

"That was when we had our canoe race," Ashley admitted.

"See?" Joy said. "I told you."

I nodded. Joy *was* telling the truth.

"Thanks, Sally," I said. "Ashley and I have to go now."

"Okay," Sally said. "See ya!"

We waved good-bye to Joy and Sally. Then we headed back down the trail.

"No wonder they're best friends," I said.

"They're both into practical jokes!"

"But Joy isn't our culprit," I said. "And neither is Mr. Clancy or the boys from Robin Cabin. We're out of suspects!"

"So now what?" Ashley asked.

"I'm not sure," I answered. We walked together in silence. As we neared the camp, our trail crossed with another one. We turned left to head toward the main lodge.

I glanced down at the ground, thinking hard. Then I stopped short. I grabbed Ashley's arm.

"What is it?" Ashley asked.

"Check it out." I pointed to the ground in front of us. There, in the dirt, were fresh footprints. Footprints that left a pattern of diamonds!

"They're just like the footprints at the overnight campsite!" Ashley cheered.

"Let's go," I said excitedly. "I have a feeling we're about to solve this case!"

FOLLOW THOSE
FOOTPRINTS

We carefully followed the path of the diamond-patterned footprints. They led us around the back of the main lodge, right up to a doorway.

"What's in there?" Ashley asked.

"The little office next to the kitchen," I told Ashley. "I saw it when I came inside to get the food for the cookout."

"Look," Ashley said. "The window is open. Let's listen in!"

We crouched under the window and

heard a bunch of people inside laughing.

"This is the best prank we've ever pulled!" Dave cheered.

"Yeah." Sandi laughed, too. "April, your idea for a camp curse was brilliant!"

"You guys were great, too." April chuckled. "You really had the kids believing in that legend."

Ashley and I stared at each other.

"No way," I whispered. "Our *senior counselors* are behind the curse!"

"But why?" Ashley asked.

"Your plan for wearing the bear rug was great, too, April," Mike declared. "We'll never be able to top it."

"I'm just glad everybody ran away." April laughed. "That rug was so itchy, I couldn't wait to take it off!"

"I just hope the kids are good sports when they find out they've been fooled," Sandi said.

"Don't worry. They'll understand. Pulling

a big prank is a tradition at Camp Crooked Lake. We do it every summer," Mike pointed out. "And besides, we *are* going to throw them a party when all this is over."

"Once we're done scaring them!" Dave added. Everyone laughed again.

"I've heard enough," I whispered.

"Me, too," Ashley agreed. We sneaked away from the window.

"Well, it looks like we solved the case," I said.

"Right," Ashley agreed. A sly smile spread across her face. "But the case isn't *closed*. Not yet!"

"Hey, where's Vicki?" April asked at dinner that night. "Didn't she come to the dining hall with you guys?"

"She had to get something at the cabin," Kimberly said. "She should be here any minute."

WHAM! The dining room door banged

open and Vicki burst inside. "Help!" she screamed. "Somebody, help!"

"What's wrong?" Mrs. Clancy cried.

"There's a wild animal outside!" Vicki shrieked. "And it's chasing Joy!"

April and Dave jumped up from their seats.

"Hurry!" Vicki shouted. "We have to do something!"

Vicki raced out the door. The senior counselors ran after her with the rest of us right behind them.

As we ran down the path toward the cabins, we heard another scream. Joy stumbled out of the trees. She looked terrified.

"Help!" she shrieked. She started running toward us. "It's after me!"

"What is?" April asked.

"A wolf!" Joy cried.

Owwwwooooooo! A low howl sounded from the trees.

"Everybody, back inside!" April cried.

Oooowwwwwwooo! Another howl. Louder this time. Then—

Crack! A branch snapped loudly.

I gasped and pointed into the woods. "There it is!"

"Roaaaaar!" A snarling creature lunged from the trees.

The senior counselors screamed.

"Heh, heh. Gotcha!" the creature said.

April blinked. "Mr. Clancy?"

Mr. Clancy grinned. Then he threw back his head and howled like a wolf.

"Oh, boy. That was a good one." Mr. Clancy chuckled.

The rest of the campers burst out laughing, too. The senior counselors turned and stared at us.

"Gotcha!" we all shouted.

Sandi gasped. "It was a trick!"

"Exactly," Ashley told her.

"We figured out that the curse of Camp Crooked Lake was nothing but a big prank,"

I added. "So we decided to get even."

"Uh-oh," Dave said. He glanced at the other senior counselors. "We're busted!"

Now *everyone* was laughing. Ashley and I explained how we had figured the whole thing out.

Mr. Clancy chuckled again. "I haven't had such a good time in years," he said.

Ashley nudged me. "Maybe he'll change his mind about closing the camp," she whispered.

"I hope so," I said. "I want to come back next summer!"

The senior counselors grinned and shook their heads.

"I guess we had it coming," Mike said.

"You two definitely taught us a lesson," April told us. "From now on, no more tricks. Just fun!"

Everyone cheered. Ashley and I grinned at each other. "*Now* the case is closed," she said.

Hi from both of us,

Ashley and I thought we were going to have tons of fun running one of the game booths at the Halloween carnival. But then the creepy giggling started—and everyone said the carnival was haunted!

At first we didn't buy it. But when we got scary fortunes saying that we should beware the giggling ghost, I wasn't so sure....

Are you ready for a spooky surprise? Turn the page for a sneak peek at *The New Adventures of Mary-Kate & Ashley: The Case of the Giggling Ghost.*

See you next time!

Mary-Kate Olsen   *Ashley Olsen*

A sneak peek at our next mystery...

The Case Of The
GIGGLING GHOST

"What do we do now?" I asked my sister, Ashley. Halloween was only three days away and we had to find out who was haunting the Halloween carnival before then!

"There's only one place at the carnival that we haven't searched for clues," Ashley announced. "The haunted house."

"Then let's go!" I said.

"I want to come, too," our friend Tim told us.

Our other friend, Sarah, shook her head. "I wouldn't go into that creepy house for a billion dollars," she said. "Besides, the carnival is closing for the night."

"If we hurry, we can make it," I said. "Let's move!"

Ashley, Tim, and I raced over to the haunted house.

"Sorry, guys," the boy running the haunted house said. "I'm closing up."

Tim checked his watch. "No fair. We still have a whole minute left before the carnival shuts down for the night!" he protested.

The boy smiled. "Okay. You three can be my last customers."

"Thanks," Ashley said. She headed for the entrance. Before she could reach the door, it slowly swung open.

She glanced at me as we stepped into the front hallway. Tons of old-fashioned portraits hung on the walls. They were covered with cobwebs.

"The guy in that picture is staring at me," Tim whispered. "And so is that lady."

"I know." I shivered. "It looks like all the portraits are watching us."

The door to the haunted house slammed shut behind us. "Eeek!" Ashley shrieked, jumping into the air.

"It's all fake, it's all fake," I repeated as I led the way up a long set of stairs. At the top was a door.

"Where do you think it leads?" Tim asked.

"Only one way to find out," I said, turning the knob. We stepped into what looked like a laboratory. Vials of green, orange, and blue liquid were lined up on a table. Lightning crackled inside a large clear ball.

"Do you guys hear that?" Ashley asked.

Thub-dub. Thub-dub. Thub-dub.

"It's a heartbeat!" I cried.

"And it's coming from over there!" Tim pointed to a long table at the back of the room.

I looked at the table and gasped. Something started to rise from the table. Something shimmery and white.

"It's the ghost!" Tim shouted.

The room went dark. I couldn't see anything. "Where's the ghost?" I cried.

There was a thump. Then silence. Too much silence.

"Mary-Kate—" Ashley began.

She didn't have a chance to say anything more. The giggling interrupted her. The horrible laughter of the giggling ghost!

The room's overhead lights clicked back on. I could see everything in the room clearly now.

The shimmery white ghost was gone—and so was Tim!

WIN **A MARY-KATE AND ASHLEY**
Best Friends Prize Pack!

WIN <u>TWO</u> OF EACH OF THE FABULOUS PRIZES LISTED BELOW:

One set for you, one set for your best buddy! It's twice as nice to share the prizes!

- Autographed photo of Mary-Kate and Ashley
- A complete library of TWO OF A KIND™, THE NEW ADVENTURES OF MARY-KATE AND ASHLEY™, MARY-KATE AND ASHLEY STARRING IN™, SO LITTLE TIME and SWEET 16™ book series
- Mary-Kate and Ashley videos
- Mary-Kate and Ashley music CDs
- 3 sets of Mary-Kate and Ashley dolls
- Mary-Kate and Ashley video games
- Mary-Kate and Ashley Fantasy Pack

IT COULD BE YOU!

THE NEW ADVENTURES OF MARY-KATE AND ASHLEY™
Best Friends Prize Pack Sweepstakes

OFFICIAL RULES:

1. No purchase necessary.

2. To enter complete the official entry form or hand print your name, address, age, and phone number along with the words "THE NEW ADVENTURES OF MARY-KATE & ASHLEY Win a Best Friends Prize Pack Sweepstakes" on a 3" x 5" card and mail to: THE NEW ADVENTURES OF MARY-KATE & ASHLEY Win a Best Friends Prize Pack Sweepstakes, c/o HarperEntertainment, Attn: Children's Marketing Department, 10 East 53rd Street, New York, NY 10022. Entries must be received no later than December 31, 2002. Enter as often as you wish, but each entry must be mailed separately. One entry per envelope. Partially completed, illegible, or mechanically reproduced entries will not be accepted. Sponsors are not responsible for lost, late, mutilated, illegible, stolen, postage due, incomplete, or misdirected entries. All entries become the property of Dualstar Entertainment Group, Inc., and will not be returned.

3. Sweepstakes open to all legal residents of the United States (excluding Colorado and Rhode Island) who are between the ages of five and fifteen on December 31, 2002, excluding employees and immediate family members of HarperCollins Publishers, Inc. ("HarperCollins"), Parachute Properties and Parachute Press, Inc., and their respective subsidiaries and affiliates, officers, directors, shareholders, employees, agents, attorneys, and other representatives (individually and collectively "Parachute"), Dualstar Entertainment Group, Inc., and its subsidiaries and affiliates, officers, directors, shareholders, employees, agents, attorneys, and other representatives (individually and collectively "Dualstar"), and their respective parent companies, affiliates, subsidiaries, advertising, promotion and fulfillment agencies, and the persons with whom each of the above are domiciled. Offer void where prohibited or restricted by law.

4. Odds of winning depend on the total number of entries received. Approximately 600,000 sweepstakes announcements published. All prizes will be awarded. Winner will be randomly drawn on or about January 15, 2003, by HarperEntertainment, whose decisions are final. Potential winner will be notified by mail and will be required to sign and return an affidavit of eligibility and release of liability within 14 days of notification. Prizes won by minors will be awarded to parent or legal guardian who must sign and return all required legal documents. By acceptance of prize, winner consents to the use of his or her name, photograph, likeness, and personal information by HarperCollins, Parachute, Dualstar, and for publicity purposes without further compensation except where prohibited.

5. One (1) Grand Prize Winner will win a Best Friends Prize Pack to include 2 of each of the following items: autographed photo of Mary-Kate and Ashley, THE NEW ADVENTURES OF MARY-KATE & ASHLEY book library, TWO OF A KIND book library, STARRING IN... book library, SO LITTLE TIME book library, SWEET 16 book library; MARY-KATE AND ASHLEY Fantasy Pack; MARY-KATE AND ASHLEY GIRLS' NIGHT OUT, CRUSH COURSE, POCKET PLANNER, MAGICAL MYSTERY MALL, WINNERS CIRCLE, and GET A CLUE video games; PASSPORT TO PARIS, BILLBOARD DAD, SWITCHING GOALS, YOU'RE INVITED TO MARY-KATE AND ASHLEY'S GREATEST PARTIES, YOU'RE INVITED TO MARY-KATE AND ASHLEY'S BALLET PARTY, and YOU'RE INVITED TO MARY-KATE AND ASHLEY'S SCHOOL DANCE PARTY videos; SO LITTLE TIME Mary-Kate doll, SO LITTLE TIME Ashley doll, SWEET 16 doll car, WINNING LONDON doll giftset; HOLIDAY IN THE SUN, WINNING LONDON, OUR LIPS ARE SEALED, MARY-KATE AND ASHLEY GREATEST HITS, and MARY-KATE AND ASHLEY GREATEST HITS II music CDs. Approximate retail value: $1,500.00.

6. Only one prize will be awarded per individual, family, or household. Prize is non-transferable and cannot be sold or redeemed for cash. No cash substitute is available. Any federal, state, or local taxes are the responsibility of the winner. Sponsor may substitute prize of equal or greater value, if necessary, due to availability.

7. Additional terms: By participating, entrants agree a) to the official rules and decisions of the judges, which will be final in all respects; and to waive any claim to ambiguity of the official rules and b) to release, discharge, and hold harmless HarperCollins, Parachute, Dualstar, and their affiliates, subsidiaries, and advertising and promotion agencies from and against any and all liability or damages associated with acceptance, use, or misuse of any prize received in this sweepstakes.

8. Any dispute arising from this Sweepstakes will be determined according to the laws of the State of New York, without reference to its conflict of law principles, and the entrants consent to the personal jurisdiction of the State and Federal courts located in New York County and agree that such courts have exclusive jurisdiction over all such disputes.

9. To obtain the name of the winner, please send your request and a self-addressed stamped envelope (excluding residents of Vermont and Washington) to THE NEW ADVENTURES OF MARY-KATE & ASHLEY Win a Best Friends Prize Pack Sweepstakes, c/o HarperEntertainment, Attn: Children's Marketing Department, 10 East 53rd Street, New York, NY 10022 by February 1, 2003. Sweepstakes Sponsor: HarperCollins Publishers, Inc.

Mary-Kate and Ashley'

New York Times Bestselling Book Series!

so little time

BASED ON THE HIT TV SERIES

I'
Who
YOU
Re

Chloe and Riley. . . So much to do. . . **so little time**

MEET KIMBERLY!

Winner of the Warner Home Video "You Can Be a Character in a Mary-Kate and Ashley Book" Sweepstakes

Kimberly is one of Mary-Kate and Ashley's biggest fans. She even went on a Sail with the Stars cruise with them! Kimberly has *all* the Mary-Kate and Ashley books. Her favorite ones are the TWO OF A KIND DIARIES because they are related to real-life experiences.

Kimberly lives in a New Jersey suburb with her mother, father and sister. When she's not reading Mary-Kate and Ashley books, she likes riding her bike, dancing, horseback riding, shopping, and hanging out with her friends. She's even a softball star, winning various trophies!!

After school and on weekends, Kimberly and her friends enjoy roller-blading, swimming, and going to the movies, the mall or out to dinner. She tries to catch Mary-Kate and Ashley on TV whenever possible.

Kimberly went to camp near home and danced in the camp's annual talent show with her friends. Their group—called the Honey Bunnies—won!

Congratulations, Kimberly!

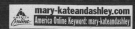